Her Infinite Search For Him

Published By

Her Infinite Search For Him

Written By Rohini Bisi

Copyright ©

Rohini Bisi - POETRY WORLD ORG 2021

ISBN (Paperback) - 9789390724574

First Edition : 2021

Book Design by POETRY WORLD

Her Infinite Search
For Him

By

Rohini Bisi

Author Bio

Myself Rohini Bishi, an engineer by profession and a writer by passion. Facing different kinds of people, a variety of situations, I have grown up to a young girl, unique as everyone is.

People grow up in a distinct environment, face variable problems and they grow up accordingly with an extraordinary character, personality, attitude and dreams, so have I.

Everyone is different and so am I. In my journey of life, me along with my mother have faced lots of struggles and battles.

In my melody of life, I have been searching for my father: my hero, everywhere at every moment of my life, and this book is just a small reflection of it.

I love traveling and find a close acquaintance with nature...

One day, I dream to be one of the best writers in the world.

JOURNEY OF VIZAG

Vishakha loves to travel. She is in college now. She is in Vizag with her mother. Vizag (Vishakhapatnam) is a beautiful clean city in Andhra Pradesh, in the lap of the Bay of Bengal. The perfectly clean, golden beach of Ramakrishna Puram, with the streamlined road along the golden sand of the brine.

The roads have captioned hoardings in Telugu and English. Vishakha booked a room facing the infinite blue waters on the fourth floor of the guest house. The little balcony of the room gave a massive view of the bay; the small hill, the rocks of the beach, and the perfectly neat city.

The foamy waves breaking on the small rocks submerged in the bay seemed as if someone was pouring soap water on the rock, giving it a spectacular view.

She wanted to visit the famous serene Rishikonda beach, Ramakrishna Ashrama, and the fish aquarium apart from the RK Puram beach.

She planned the tour along with her mother, as they love traveling and this beautiful city. This is the second time they have visited the place.

Vishakha wonders why she is so fond of traveling. Is it because of her dad, who used to love traveling, and made two tours in a year mandatory?

She hardly knows her father. The only things that she knows are of a 3-year kid's memory and the facts that her mother narrated to her.

A father is a daughter's first love, and superhero. A daughter gets familiar with the opposite gender through her father. The love, warmth, protection, and care that is attributed by a father, leads to the formation of the character of the daughter, from a kid to a teenager and finally an adult.

The way a girl is treated by her father from childhood, the very same way she will treat the world. And those who don't know their father at all? What about them? They will keep searching for their father frantically in every corner of the world.

Their eyes will search for the pair of eyes which would be filled with the father's pure love which is unintentional and unconditional. She feels she is the reflection of her dad and it is her responsibility to enact her dad. The work a dad does, she should be doing it. In this birth, in this journey of life, she will feel her dad in this very method.

ESCAPE FROM THORNS

She was just a kid when she lost her father. She still used to talk to her father. She felt that her father did not leave her and is with her constantly.

It was a full moon night; she was 5 years old then. She and her mother were returning home from her school friend's house. A big thorny dry branch of a tree was lying in the middle of the road which they didn't notice. They were walking fast which trapped them. They got stuck and didn't know what to do. They tried to get out of the vicious trap but failed. The little terrified Vishakha started calling her father for help. She just called her dad to rescue her and her mother. She knew her dad had to come to rescue them. He can't be so selfish and ignorant about his duty to protect them. Slowly some magic occurred.

The thorns appeared to respect them, and they were trying their best to get it out. Slowly, they were out after struggling for 30 minutes. They went back home, thanking God and the little kid thanked her father too, who was there always with her.

She used to cry a lot for her father and even now she cries a lot. She remembers her father carrying her on his shoulders and walking around the house slowly. She remembers her father making boats for her, buying chocolates and balloons upon her demand. The evening walks with her father, where she is looking at the world with her little eyes from her father's shoulder and she is holding her father's head firmly with her little hand is still like a clear picture to her.

She remembers the walk to nursery school with her papa and him carrying her on his lap, lest her legs would hurt. She would walk like a carefree kid, like a little diva.

Parents are the protectors of a kid. A family has a father, a mother, and a child. A father takes care of the child and the mother.

LOVE FOR ACADEMICS

As Vishakha grows up, she spends more time with her academic books. She learns how her mother has sacrificed her job, only to give her a secure, tension-free environment.

She learns how her mother gives the lion's share of the food to nourish her and herself eating less. She learns how her mother arranges everything she needs, starting from food, clothing, books, and transportation. It's not easy for a woman to become both a mother and a father.

Her health slowly gets weaker due to stress and lack of proper nutrition. Many people advise her mother to marry her off just when she completes 18 as she is a fatherless child. But her mother supports her dream of studying B.tech and rejecting the proposal of getting married a second time, mainly thinking about her well being.

All of this triggers a dream of excelling in academics. She was quite shy and different from her friends in her childhood and teenage. She studied in a girl's school. She thought she will not run after those who don't pay heed to her rather she would focus on her career. Her mother always says one thing, "Stand on your own feet! That's all I want! I am doing all these efforts only to raise you!"

She feels her pain and struggle. She excels in her academics, especially in mathematics. She always used to get maximum marks in maths. Everyone used to tell her she learns Mathematics, but she knew she loves it.

Why she loves mathematics?

Why does she want to be an engineer?

Why she gives academics a special place?

Does all this have some connection with her dad? Is it the genes and blood of her father that provokes her to have special love and affection for mathematics and chemistry?

She keeps searching for her father in her academics. She feels by being more attentive, she is coming closer to her dad and making him happy. After every good result, she feels, of her dad if he would see such marks he would be so joyous, indeed he is always watching. While all girls bullied her for how she got good marks in science and maths, the answer was simple, study and practice.

Her good marks always made her mother happy that her hard work is reaping. She lived in her world during her early teenage. She was a favourite student of most of her teachers, while many teachers scolded her for not scoring so well in other subjects as in mathematics.

Though she was able to score 90+ in every subject in her 10th boards, making the school proud, the happiest person is her mother. Both of them missed her dad, as in pre-nursery school he said, "This time she stood second, next time she would stand first!" Yes, she stood first and kept his words.

Her father said once to her mother, "I will teach her maths and science in class 9 and 10!"

This very statement made her leave tuition for maths and science in class 9. After attending 2 months class, she felt she took a great risk and her decision to study own by her school teacher's guidance and yes, of course, her father was guiding all through to succeed.

Many said the teachers loved her so she stood with such marks but her hard work got reflected in her flawless answer sheets. One teacher remarked, "No one can touch her maths answer sheet. Not a single mistake and in economics, she is scoring so low."

The same was reported to her mother at parent-teacher meetings, but Vishakha made it on the boards.

She looked so childish. People found it difficult to believe that she was such a studious student and did so well in academics. But she did it. Life began after class 10 and took a new turn.

After every good result, she cried for her dad, and she cries now also very silently.

HER LOVE FOR FOOD

Vishakha's father had to struggle in his childhood. He had to take tuitions from college life to meet the needs of money. So he always worried about his source of income. His father was a great cook and food lover. He cooked every dish very deliciously.

Vishakha tries to copy his style by making rich dishes with help of her mother and google search. Her father being an excess foodie and street food lover, ruined his health slowly, finally bringing devastation in her and her mother's life.

Vishakha has the habit of gulping phuchka, chop, chat, pakora, egg rolls, and other junk foods. She loves sweets and chocolate just like her father. Vishakha's mother is worried about her health status and keeps warning her. She says she will control but jumps into chewing some pakora instead. She started a lot of these from her college days as a result of stress and passion. Being overweight and obedient to her mother she didn't have any junk food in her childhood but in college, when her mother's health deteriorated she began this habit.

One day, she thinks she can control her thirst for junk food. She tries to copy her father in every way, but she should leave the bad and strain out the best traits to be the best version of her dad.

MARKETING

Since the age of seventeen, Vishskha started shopping which her mother always does. She feels in general, the man of the house does all of his office job and marketing like bringing vegetables, fruits, fishes, eggs, chicken, grocery, and everything which a household needs. The woman takes care of the cooking and all household chores but her mother has been doing the task of both man and woman of the house, father and mother for her, neglecting her food habits, her health for a long time which resulted in deterioration of her health.

Vishakha then took the responsibility of the 'man of the house' and she always related herself to the story 'man of the house' written by Frank O'Connor, which she read in class 9 in a school English book. The story touched her heart and she somewhere found similarity with the 10-year-old Sullivan.

She took up the responsibility of marketing, arousing other's curiosity, why the daughter is doing all the household chores and the mother is staying at home. She felt to reply when questioned by an uncle or aunty, that which lady of the house goes on doing such work unless and until there's some urgency?

Women love shopping but not all do. Many do for the sake of necessity. For some it's a passion, some it's a habit and for some it's a necessity. She likes doing marketing, though she is bad at bargaining.

She looked like a boy when she started marketing. Her mother was very sick then. She never allowed her to cook or do shopping since her childhood. Vishakha somewhat took this as her duty.

Uncles got stunned. She started exploring the city from her nearest shop to the farthest. People understood a small kid has come, she can be made a fool. She got cheated several times, with stale fish or eggs or rotten fruits and dry vegetables. She was asked for a higher price. She did not know how to bargain, slowly learned yet not efficient. She started exploring a variety of seasonal fruits and vegetables.

Initially, her mother used to cry that she is doing the household chores which she never thought of but then started helping her by giving tips and tricks. Till then she missed her dad but from then on she started feeling what the responsibilities of a father are. She went to the same market where he used to. 'Cause, it was the place where things could be bought together systematically. Just like everything under one roof which are required for day to day life.

SOCIETY

Vishakha's mother, being a widow, with no make-up, with the whole burden of a family and a little kid, even at a young age, people thought her of more age.

She hardly had proper food. She looked sick. The symbols of a married woman hide their age. Vishakha did not like to talk to people, liked to stay aloof as she grew up. What people would avoid her, being a fatherless child?

People thought they are helpless, would ask for help, so many avoided them. She avoided them. She began to enjoy studies and solitude. Her ideologies were different, mentality didn't match with others. She found abstract ideas more precious. Yes, the basic needs of life are required but they can give us comfort, not happiness. But love, friendship, care, respect, sympathy, originality, and spiritualism are abstract things that she valued more.

She found most people materialistic with fewer emotions.

She failed to be practical or reasonable as society wanted. People studied for money and jobs. She too needed a job more than anyone, but she studied because she loved it.

She feels, she is not fit for society, but as she grew up, she met people, though very few, who were much like her. They encouraged her, appreciated her, and liked her strange yet sober nature which makes her feel that she is special.

She has fewer relatives, so she treats her friends as her relatives.

MARRIAGE

People marry because they have to marry, and they dream of it. Parents think girls have to get married at a good house, the moment they are born. It's their big headache till they are not wedded to a decent family. They adjust because they are bound by responsibility and social rules. Not everyone is truly happy.

Vishakha has grown up seeing her mother wholly single. Vishakha has never thought of getting married, except to stand on her own feet. During her teenage, whenever the topic of boys was discussed among friends, she stayed away from them. Later, she had a lot of friends who slowly removed her fear by saying that, they too are human beings, not aliens.

Father's friendship and not having even close male cousins were the reasons. She was misunderstood by many of her friends because people find it difficult to believe simple and innocent things. She respects men and treats them the same as a woman because everyone is first a human being, has a soul then comes the matter of gender. Her school friends thought about how she would adjust to a co-ed environment, how she would study in a co-ed college, how she would work at the office. But she studied in a co-ed college being an alien. And finally, she thought of marriage!

Yes! Not being grown up in a happily married family, and not seeing a happy marriage has affected her deeply. She has seen her mom all alone struggling as a single parent. She has full of tensions. But there is happiness in being single.

For her, marriage is a boundary that she regards but she thinks having a successful marriage is not everyone's cup of tea. She doesn't know whether one should force oneself to it. Can she love marriage?

Girls should be solely independent. Then only they can think of marriage as a choice and marry according to their specifications and liking. The ultimate destination of love is marriage. She agrees with it. But many people are still scared of it.

In between the war of searching for her father's friendship and her disinterest in marriage, she is confused. Finally, will she end up ruining her life by forcing herself into marriage, by changing her basic interest, or stay happy forever? People think not getting married, is being insecure, weak, and an omen for society. They speak, "You have to get married, you are brought to this earth for so." As if that is the only work left.

She respects the thought, it is important, but one can't force to get married. People think being single is worse than being a divorcee but it will ruin two people's lives and even two families.

PLATONIC

Platonic love is very rare on this earth, but it is what she earns to fulfill the friendship of her dad. Vishakha was thinking about love, friendship, and expectations.

Is expectation always needed? No, not necessary.

People can't link marriage to happiness, as even after marriage people aren't happy. Love marriages are ending in divorce in 6 or a few months. So not only her, few people on earth, who are not interested in marriage, should think twice before taking any step towards it. 'Everyone is marrying, so should one...' This thought can change one for a while temporarily, but not in the long term.

So self-studying, analyzing, and judging is very important. People depict marriage as a celebration. Indeed, it is! But marriage should be treated as optional and not mandatory, as per Vishakha's thinking. She thinks if she forces herself it can lead to disaster ruining not one but two lives.

Demands and expectations often ruin everything. But that is ruling every relationship on earth, right? You fulfill the needs of people, even if it's only giving company by simply talking or gossiping. You are giving time to someone. Means giving something i.e time, which is not going to return.

Love without expectations or demands. When there are fewer chances of unity in the future, it is relevant. But when there are chances of getting unity, if we drop out the fact that, "This should be done, then it shall work, else not."

Means staying together for some expectations. Now, zero expectations for our beloved are not possible. But keeping it to a minimum or at least not making it conditional "Do this, then I am with you, else not!"

Lots of understanding and concern is needed. The feeling of independence is required in both. I will be free and give freedom too. Again, trust issue arises. Trust is a pillar for bonding. No trust, no peace. And trust is to be kept by both.

Respect for each other's individuality is needed. The jealous feeling of other's success ruins the relationship. Suppression of talent can lead to a split-up of love. There are a lot of boundaries on us from before, we don't want further shackles.

So whether marriage or relationship, there should be freedom within boundaries. Free to accept individuality, identity and visions.

Good friends keep no expectations or demands. So, the spouse should be made friend first. Share everything, explain everything and understand. But not everyone turns out to be friendly or understanding. Love depends on destiny too. So, it's the magic of love we should depend on.

So, Vishakha feels what she earns is the best, that is platonic love because it has minimum expectations.

UNIQUE

Vishakha always knew since childhood, that she is different from others and she believes that everyone is unique on this earth. She listened to a motivational speech of her favorite personality where he explained so beautifully the value of oneself. Everyone is special, has some quality where they are promising.

Vishakha always hated comparison still she excelled. She never felt low. Others compared their marks with hers and now also she faces competition which does not hold any meaning. People feel depressed when someone is greater than them and superior when they are greater than others.

Vishakha always felt good things can be learnt from others but not compared. She always compared herself with herself. She judged what she was, how much she scored before, and now what she is, how much she is scoring now.

She feels everyone is unique, every single person has a different talent and everyone has a separate life. One factor can't decide the status of accomplishment and prosperity in life. Everyone is sent on the earth for a special reason or utility. Society expects the same actions for everyone to make them settled.

Amongst everything, we forget to be happy. Self-love, self-care, self-time is almost forgotten in this running world. We do our duties and forget to think about our mental peace and tranquility.

There should be a balance between our actions to live and actions for us. If we aren't happy, then we can't keep others happy. Vishakha was so different from others, that she had fewer friends in school. Initially, she was sad, later she became ignorant about it. She remained a kid and her innocent nature did become a reason for attraction.

She missed her father and wondered had he been now, how would have been the bonding between them. Would he take her to tuitions and school like she watches others? Would he spend time listening to her problems and solve them?

Would he share all his liking, disliking, and memories of childhood? All these thoughts bring tears to her eyes.

Her situation and the care her mother have taken of her made her a different person altogether. She has grown up to a naive and simple girl. Simply, she is a unique human being searching for her father's friendship.

DREAMS FULFILLED

Her father is a descendant of some famous writer but he was a chemical engineer from Jadavpur University. She always wanted to be part of JU. But she could not make a good rank in WBJEE. But she wanted to be an engineer to follow the footsteps of her dad.

She told her mother, "I didn't understand my Dad, I want to learn about his profession" but she forgot about her gender that core industries are really difficult for girls to work in.

She wanted to be a part of the core industry in her professional life just to feel like her father. She forgot her father is always with her whether she would be a teacher or an engineer. She loved maths and chemistry just for her father.

She thought of honors in maths or chemistry because of her talent in maths but she had to walk in the path of her father. So, she opted to be an engineer and left biology in class 11. So that by mistake also she doesn't become a doctor because her mother's paternal uncle, paternal grandfather, and paternal great grandfather were all famous doctors.

Her mother wanted to be a doctor but for certain circumstances, she could not be. Her mother could not do masters because of early marriage and no support from her family. So, she always wanted her daughter to do whatever she wants and never enforced her to do anything.

Vishakha's father could not pursue M.Tech. Vishakha decided that after exhausting all of their savings in B.Tech if she pursued a masters it would only be done if she qualified GATE. After she qualified she got the scholarship and she fulfilled her dream of studying in a scholarship which she always deserved, her mother's dream of her becoming an engineer got fulfilled after PG.

At last but not least she fulfilled her father's wish also. Now she wants to remain alive forever by writing and though she may not be renowned like her ancestors, she can at least try to reach a few steps further. Karma or duty is immortal; it is just how far and how your good deeds are spread.

How you benefit the world, what steps you take and which methods are adopted. Vishakha feels a human birth is precious, she has got after overcoming how many births, she doesn't know.

She is not aware of her past actions but all she knows is her present birth and duty. So after struggling so much she doesn't want this birth to go to waste. She wants to write and write till she becomes the best one.

ALWAYS A GROWN UP

Vishakha's father was born in Rajkot. Vishakha was in class 3 when she and her mother went on a tour to Gujarat with a reputed tour and travel package. There she felt her father's special presence as they crossed Rajkot. Her mother has been always insecure about her safety but a break was required for their stressful life, so they went to quite a few places along with trustworthy people.

Vishakha and her mother both loved traveling. Vishakha was overweight in her childhood so she looked more aged compared to her actual age. But she was overloaded with the innocence of a kid half of her age and maturity that of a double aged person.

People whenever met her mother said only one thing, "Your daughter has grown up!" When she was in class 5 or 8 or 10. From class 10 people thought she was in class 6! That was a great transformation and when she was in college she looked like a 10-year little boy!

She missed being a child. Though her mother always treats her as a kid, the world was not good for her. A child should be treated as a kid and not as an adult.

So she stayed away. After a long time, she met a man, who treated her as a kid and she started searching for the reflection of her father in him. Though he was much younger than her father, she started searching for the friendship of his dad in him. Earlier than this she searched in every male friend she talked to and remarked them as her father too, for listening to her talks, problems and hilarious jokes.

But this person was really special as he did say, if he had a daughter, she would have been like her. But she knows her real father is always with her. He is there holding her hands, even if she tumbles down with her little shaky legs.

Even if she falls he will lift her and protect her. She can't miss her dad, because he is always with her. When she is sad and cries out loud, he wipes her tears and swings her in the air to make her giggle again. He is always there with her though she has grown up.

BEGINNING OF DARKNESS

A normal active young man, an expert as a cook, and greatly obsessed with food, brought disaster into his young pretty wife and her newborn kid. A little bit cautious about health and following a healthy routine would have made their lives a less miserable one.

Everyone has struggled, every family does have suffering but if their father would be with them their suffering would be shared by three instead of getting overloaded on two. Vishakha wonders if she had her father now, how she would behave.

Would she help him in his regular work like cooking or marketing? Would she argue with him on mathematics and engineering topics? Would she share all her topics as she does with her mom?

Would she take care of his health? Would she scold him for his wrongdoings and vice versa? Would she get married off by her father against her will? Would he play indoor games and feel superior in defeating her dad?

Would she teach him about new trends of technology? Would she demand her favorite things from her dad? What would she call her dad by, Baba, Papa, Bapi, or Dad?

All these questions keep reckoning her. The answers are blurred because she doesn't know what it would be.

PRECIOUS RELATIONSHIP

The relationship between a daughter and her father is one of the most beautiful relationships on the earth. The quality of this relationship defines the character, nature, and attitude of the girl and the mental state of the father's daily life.

The more love and happiness between a daughter and her dad, the lesser the problems faced by the girl in the world. The relationship of a dad and his girl builds her personality and temperament for life.

Vishakha didn't have her dad in person but only in her imagination. So, she kept searching her father. She didn't have male friends of her age from childhood till college. So in every uncle she talked to she searched for her dad and sometimes she behaved as if they were her father for some time only.

She was close to only some of them, chatting freely, sharing food and asking stupid questions as every girl does to a dad. One of them was her friend's dad whom she was sacred of, like a strict dad he was! In college, she was very shy and hardly talked to any guy leaving those who talked to her on their own.

She had few male friends then. After graduation, she got a smartphone and WhatsApp with her scholarship money! Then she talked to guys from her college, colony and some unknown from facebook too. She was decent, respectful, friendly, and innocent with everyone she talked to. But the world doesn't appreciate good things and want to ruin them or capture them.

She kept on searching for her father's platonic love and friendship.

Few were good but most of them were not. She faced problems, learned, got hurt, and then understood finally, "No one in this world can be her Dad!" Nor can anyone give his love, protection, and friendship. She has a few good friends whom she treasures.

INTERACTION

Vishakha's aunt once said to her mother, after a few days Vishakha will forget her father. Even many of her friends in school asked her, "Do you remember anything about your father? Do you recall your father? Have you seen your father?"

Questions like these always hurt her. Yes, but she can't blame someone else for this. Maybe it's quite normal. But every tinge of her life, every corner of her existence is filled with her dad. With every breath she takes, she knows she does not have her father, and she and her mother form the family.

After college life, she did have many male friends mostly communicated through social and digital media. She kept on searching for her father's friendship. Isn't it normal for her? But it was all useless! For a girl to grow normal, a good healthy relationship with her dad is required to know how she would face the opposite gender.

She was very friendly, respected them, listened to their problems, tried to solve them as far as she could but her softness became poison for her. Some tried to take advantage of her being too good, some gave their best version. But now after talking to so many people she realized, it's one of the most stupid things she did in her life.

Her mother is correct, "No one can be your dad, it's just a waste of time and energy!"

She searched for nothing much, not money but attention, protection, respect, and trust. She did get quite a few worthy and precious friends to be treasured for life but there were few, those who gave her the only lesson "Don't be too good, don't be Mother Teresa, don't be so self-less, learn to think about yourself first."

Her nature was quite soft and innocent not fit for the world which attracted many. But finally, she realized it's better to be in her den than to accompany the wrong herd. Interacting with the world was not working, so she decided to interact with her inner self and indulge in creativity which keeps the mind and soul happy and fresh.

DEVOTION

Vishakha is a great devotee of Lord Shiva since childhood and she calls Him her own father though He is not only her father but of the universe! She calls the lord her 'baba' with love and affection since childhood. As she grew up, she attained an affection for Lord Krishna, she read the Gita and tried to grasp the meaning of life.

She seeks protection and knows very well nothing is happening without the will of the Almighty. As per the words of Lord Ramakrishna, a leaf cannot move without His will. He is one and all religions are methods to worship Him.

She feels Lord Krishna will save her from all problems in her life as He kept saving Prahlad when he was thrown from the highest cliff, set ablaze, and put in all kinds of dangers. Vishakha believes in prarabdha karma, the actions of previous birth. She initially thought all activities going on are the result of actions in this birth, but when her college friend remarked about her childhood events regarding her father, she changed her thoughts.

Indeed, the Lord has said too, prarabdha is predominating our lives at every instant. The bhagya or fortune or luck are all bestowed with actions or deeds. So she thinks, better let me do the karma, join my hands, pray to the Almighty and leave results on Him.

He is the father of the universe and will take care of us.

ARMOUR

It's 7 pm. Dark all around. Vishakha is pacing fast, through the dark lane. After walking a distance, she looks back at the lonely dark street, the distance she covered. With big, tall trees on both sides of the lane, the LED street lights gives a conical beam of light on the road, brightening the path.

An unknown sensation triggers in her beating heart. She looks up at the sky, the navy-blue color of the atmosphere, sprinkled with glittering stars and a cool breeze gives her the feeling that she is not alone. Someone is there. Yes of course! The Almighty is watching over her! But along with Him, she calls upon her father secretly.

"You have to be with me, baba! You have to be there always with me, till every breath I take! You can't run away from your responsibility; you have to take care of me!"

A soothing silent faithful answer whispered into her ears, "I am always there with you, don't worry my dear child!" Vishakha smiled at herself silently.

A teardrop of sadness and happiness came into her eyes. Isn't it natural?

"On a lonely street, when I walk, you have to be my armor!" She wonders if her father would have been with her today, she might have studied in a different place, a different life, a different lifestyle! Although she doesn't know about the consequences, they would be in a much better and safer point of life.

She feels too insecure at times and feels lost in the middle of the sea, boarded in a ship with no compass, or in the middle of an illusionary forest which has no path to escape or trapped in a dark cave with the entrance and exit closed.

She feels to cry and scream at such perilous times of her life. Then she feels that her father is her invisible armor which she can't see but can only feel with pure love and faith.

LOVE AND HATE

Can you love and hate a person at the same time? Yes, very strange but it's possible. Since childhood, she only had love for her dad but as she grew up she realized all the problems they face and all the sufferings are because of a male guardian.

If she had her father, her mother would be fit and fine and their life would be far better and different from their present miserable condition. The 4 years of B.Tech went in realization and she got a hatred that why wasn't he little careful regarding his eating habits and lifestyle which lead to their destruction.

So a mixture of love and agony arose within her towards her loving dad. It's true that she still loves him the most but hates him for making their conditions worse. God is the only abode for such helpless people.

The fear, problems, humiliation, and anxiety which encircles her always is because of her father. If she had her father now, she would be tension free and lead an entirely different life. Theirs would be a perfect trio home!

EMOTIONALLY WEAK

Though Vishakha's friends say that she is very strong, she feels she is emotional and the weakest. After climbing many mountains of barrier and overcoming them, she is still weak and has an excess of sympathy which is bound to get misunderstood and misused.

She has always tried to help others and has listened to their problems empathetically. This has lead her to trouble, because people tend to overuse good things. But she always knew her limits and had to warn people when they did cross their limits and sometimes left their path, leading to breakage of friendship.

What can she do, if she is different? She knows very well things can be bought of the same type, but human beings can never have a copy. Never! She keeps searching for a unique person in the herd of a variety of people, which is just next to impossible till the Almighty sends one!

This reminds her of some people she has seen in Haridwar, searching for coins in the holy river Ganga. The water there is crystal clear, with some part directed to a certain bank for the facility of tourists and devotees. The speed and amount of water is less in this particular region which enables the coin searchers to walk in the river and search for coins with glass. People throw coins in the river, which lies visible mixed with the pebbles.

The view excited Vishakha and she saw how people struggle for existence. Everyone on this earth struggles for existence.

LIFE IS A GAME

Vishakha saw a little girl aged seven or eight on a bike, sitting behind her father. The bike was standing and the father was wearing a helmet that was not properly worn by her father. The little girl with her little hands was telling him repeatedly, "Wear the helmet properly, Dad!"

Vishakha's eyes got filled with water. She felt would she take care of her dad's minute needs? Would she supervise her Dad's health? Would she ensure that her Dad would not gulp in street food randomly and have a regular exercise schedule? She feels so messy. What was her fault?

She wonders if it's because of her past birth actions she is suffering. She is unlucky to not have the love of her father but her father is unlucky too not to have the affection of a daughter! Life is a game of karma that is beyond the power of her understanding and knowledge.

She is a tiny human being, ignorant of the infinite truth, bows down to the Almighty, the creator, the controller, and the preserver of the Universe!

What is going to happen in the next moment no one knows. She prefers to stay in present and be what she is. Life is too short to follow others and be like what others want you to be.

Since childhood, she sometimes feels, she is lost in a dense magical forest at midnight with no escape route, thorns around and the hooting sound of wild animals around, with only a blissful ray of hope guiding her path like that of heaven!

The always nagging child suddenly had no demands since the point she realized, she and her mother are without a father, a guardian, an armor, a roof. Vishakha is a combination of a little kid and a mature person.

Her innocence is still like a kid and maturity is like that of a grown-up. The kid is herself and the maturity belongs to whom? Is it the situation? Or is it her father alive within her like a protector?

STAYED DIFFERENT

Vishakha's mother is a beautiful young lady who suddenly grew old. Evergreen lady turned to an anxious widow. Everyone remarked previously about her perfect yet simple makeup. Her dressing style and matching combo made everyone envy her.

Now, she never put on a single makeup, wore a light-colored saree, no matching combination, never thought about her health or food habits always engrossed in anxiety and not a single makeup.

Vishakha grew up seeing her simple, sweet, naturally beautiful mother so she too prefers to be simple and natural. Yes, she does put on make-up but tries to limit, because she is a believer of the fact, simple living high thinking.

She could not make friends in childhood. Because of her so different nature, she made academics her best friend in school. Although she hardly had any friends, there were some gems in her life with whom she has contact and some she remembers in her heart.

Her school life wasn't that boring as other school friends thought. She used to spend maximum time practicing mathematics. She spent even three to four days on a single problem until it got solved.

Mathematics was her passion though people spread rumors about how she used to mug up. Is it possible to mug up maths numerical? If it is, she doesn't know then.

She spent hours on this special subject. She loved chemistry too. Was she so much interested in science and maths to get good marks to make her mother smile? Or along with it, she kept on searching for her Dad?

She keeps searching for her father in every bit of her life, in every action she does, in every moment of her life! Her father was a good athlete, a good table tennis player and played cricket with her at home when she was a kid.

She can't be such a good athlete, never played table tennis, but she always dreamt of working in core industries.

MISTAKES

People can't forget their failures in life. They keep on repenting and stay engrossed in it. They feel they are great sinners. Vishakha was listening to a motivational video. It was very encouraging as well as interesting.

He said how he made the mistake of pouring excess lemon while making lemonade and it was too sour to have it. So he added extra water and made 4 times the lemonade from the same amount of lemon juice. Now, similarly if by mistake we add excessive salt to a dish or sweet to kheer we can't take out the salt or sugar or lemon which is already added. What is done is done!

But we can surely add extra water to the lemonade or extra vegetables in the dish or extra rice to the kheer and increase the amount and correct the fault of the dish. Similarly, if we make one mistake that we believe was not to be done, it can't define us.

Our definition comes from everything we do in our life! We can't know or judge ourselves from one mistake! But we can surely improve our life by taking the lesson seriously. We can do so much good work to dilute the fault, that the fault seems to be a miniature.

The mistake or failure was harmful to us, in the process of knowing or judging ourselves. But that is not everything in all. That is not the only thing we have in our life.

For example, we fail to judge a person; a masked person probably. We ignore our inner voice, we fail. That should be a lesson. We should make so many good friends that one wrong person won't judge our life.

Vishakha also made mistake in judging people and suffered emotionally, but she took the lesson from each person and moved forward by becoming stronger and more reserved. She slowly changed to one which was the older version of her with better attributes.

FACING PEOPLE

The world is illusionary. Nothing here is permanent! Only the Supreme power or energy is!

Vishakha keeps ego at bay and hugs innocence and simplicity! She treats all humans with respect and expects respect back. She is close to very few selective people. She never boasts of herself which has lead her to problems. A little ego is required, to maintain self-dignity, but that should not make someone proud unnecessarily.

Being low, humble, gentle is good because ego is worthless, as we are all children of the Almighty. But don't be so low that people will break you down. Many times, people have treated her like no one, not humans; she faced criticism and had been made fun of, mostly because of their situation and being extraordinary.

Many friends turned to strangers after their tragedy. People remain young and evergreen with people around but when they have to face the battle alone they become mature, old, strong, and sensible. God gives troubles to those who act to be heroic and keeps those in cradle those who act like 'they can't do anything'. But when you are in a better position you will get many good wishes and acknowledgments.

They were kept aloof and neglected in society except few who understood their struggle and gave them respect. They had to become ignorant about people else they would become depressed.

Slowly, when Vishakha became a good student, and the news spread, people used to watch her with wonder, some became happy and congratulated her. But, no there were critics too!

People find out the flaws of the most perfect things on this earth, so would she be left out? She is just a common ordinary person! How can she be left out? How is she getting so many marks? The answer is simple, hard work!

But yes, some remarked she must be studying 24 hours a day! Oh no! She is a human being, she too has her limits, and it's not always the quantity but quality that matters. Your level of concentration and understanding matters. Vishakha started being less worried about people's conversations because she can't keep on explaining how she made things work, what was her time management. No one can copy someone, as everyone is different, has a different life and composition.

Everyone has their own life, worth, and virtue. Source, route, and destination of success for each, and everyone is varied and not common. So people should start studying about themselves, learn good qualities from others, and stop comparing with others.

She heard from a motivational video, that people compare with others when they aren't happy with themselves, so they grumble. Vishakha can't help though people asked her to change!

Let it be herself, her circumstances, her childhood, her life and all these factors made her unique, out of the common league. She tried to change only landing to hurt herself.

She understood changing would lead her to destroy her soul, her inner being, which she can't afford to live!

THIRD SEAT

On the morning train to Kolkata, whenever she and her mother travels, she feels the third seat of theirs is occupied by an outsider. One day suddenly a thought strikes her that if her father had been today, the third seat would be occupied by him and their life would also not be devastated!

Every journey she has, she feels her father's presence because of the love he had for traveling. Her mother often tells, 'how are you so systematic in packing and managing things?' She replies, 'I learned from you, mom.'

Her mother replies, 'You are more systematic than me!' Vishakha thinks maybe her father is working through her to help them!

'Your father is always with you, can never leave you!', one of her friends remarked when she was shattered due to her problems. She shared with her friends how she missed him. Every moment she feels father is with them yet not there. She gets upset and cries silently, yelling at her father for their problem.

Sometimes she feels she has grown up so much and moved ahead, again next moment she feels she is at the same point of life and has not moved an inch forward!

On her tour to Guwahati and one day visit to Shillong, when an abrupt change in the weather occurred and the road they had taken to Cherrapunji, was covered with a long stretch of clouds, she felt their life too had the same change years ago.

You aren't prepared, suddenly, all of the sunshine disappears. Your path is covered with clouds and you can see nothing but only white fog all around. No sunray to break the moisture and make the path clear. On one side lies the East Khasi Hills and on the other deep trench with dense forest, with small waterfalls in between whose rumbling sounds can be heard!

What they could see was only the one-foot distance in front of the slow-moving car, with headlights on at 12 o clock in the daylight. Vishakha and her mother were silent and not said a word so that the concentration of the driver would not be hampered by the slightest. They just watched the view, the pine trees and green sober mountains disappeared suddenly. In their place came the howling speedy winds with white fog looking more like smog. She stopped the car went to see the Umiam lake, had Maggie but a cloud came and hugged her giving a cold shock!

After returning from Cherrapunji, in a bad mood, as they couldn't see an inch of the Gorgeous Seven Sister Falls, she could see the spectacular landscape of Shillong, with green fields, a variety of species of trees hanging from mountains, small huts as sunshine has smiled on the Queen hill station and fog had to fly away.

The view of Seven Sister falls was covered with a thick layer of fog and clouds. Nature had its play; she could not see a trace of it but hearing only the rapid sound of seven waterfalls.

Nature didn't return her empty-handed as she had the experience of the clouds covering their path, locking their vision only to a feet distance, teaching a lesson, that focusing on the present and keeping no expectations will lead to a beautiful future with unexpected positive surprises.

INFINITE SEARCH

Boys search mothers in their wives, can't girls search for fathers in their husbands? Whenever she asked the question of searching father in a life partner, the male friend replied, it's not possible!

In every male friend, she searched for her father, which is very absurd. Nothing only the company, friendship, empathy and care a friend can give which a father gives to her princess as a friend.

'Mom, I am searching for my Dad!'

'Dear, this is vague. You are never going to be successful! No one can be your Dad! It's a very special and sensitive place which no one ever can take!'

Vishakha got disheartened and found it hard to believe. But slowly with time and more people she befriended, she learned her mother's words are right. No one can take the place of her Dad. It's a very delicate and precious relationship. She stopped searching for her Dad because she feels he is with her always and she has wasted time, efforts, and energy in searching for him anywhere else. She was good as a kid; crying, talking, laughing, complaining, and loving her baba the way she did.

Her father scolded her in nursery school to not go after people who didn't pay heed to her. Maybe she didn't change only after learning lessons. After growing up, talking to so many people, learning about them, she realized her father told her right and she was introvert in childhood that was the best version!

People either use or fail to understand you except the jewel ones, who will understand you always! Every person she talked to gave her a lesson and so not wasting time! She has a bad habit of knowing people, learning about their problems, and trying to solve them. This habit of being 'too good' has lead her to problems leaving her distaste for any new friends and likes to stick to the old ones!

Her infinite search for her father in people ended but not in every moment, every place and every action of her life!

UNCERTAIN LIFE

Who will know better than her that life is very uncertain? Well everyone knows it, and the coronavirus has made everyone realize so.

The year 2020 was a tragic year for everyone on this earth because of this undefeatable, indomitable product of nature.

Nature can take such a ravaging form; the corona has set another example. Why should she waste time trying to change herself for the happiness of others? She should focus on what makes her happy!

She feels to do something genuine which will make her remember for ages and set an example of inspiration. Well, karma makes one immortal; yes it just depends on how many people remember your good deeds. She sees people celebrating the success of great men and women.

She wonders about the formula, there are no tips or tricks at all. The formula is simple continuous efforts, excelling, having a proper ground to perform, and most importantly, the blessing of the Supreme!

What can she do to be the one? She thinks how can she be an achiever? What is she good at? Her father's ancestors had been great writers; she loves to write but not a prolific one.

She sometimes thinks about why she chose to be an engineer and could be a mathematics professor. It could be better for her as she is a girl and the engineering field and working in the core industry is tough!

But no, she had to walk in the footsteps of her father, to understand his profession if not him. She had to keep the tag of 'Engineer' in her life, to feel her papa.

Strange! And sometimes she feels she is weird to think of it but is she feeling it? The third seat of her family?

BEING OR DOING

Again, a motivational video triggered a question in her mind. What is she doing in her life? Is she a human being or a human doing?

She found it difficult to trust people since childhood but when she put her steps into the world she thought every human being to be an angel which cost her a lot of pain, anxiety, and agony. Resulting she lost trust in people once again but not humanity.

But the concept of a human being means being humanly, raised her mind to ask her questions, is she only going on working or doing all the time?

Or does she retrospect her life, herself, and her soul? As the physical body needs nourishment the soul also needs nutrition and care. How is she going to take care of her soul? Some me time when she thinks about her wants, likes, or dislikes, or looks at nature with awe, studies the psychology of people she watches around, the life where everyone is racing to save themselves and their family.

When she thinks of life she is being and when she performs she is doing. Is there a balance between her being and doing? Is her soul getting nourished? What entity will help her to know if there is a perfect balance between the two?

Yes, there is an entity! The level of tranquility in her life will define it. People find peace in various activities, some in devotion, some in meditation, and some in others.

Life is uncertain as well as precious. We get this human birth; let it not go to waste! We have life and then we have everything else, academics, money, job, success, and happiness. Life is a gift itself!!

So, let us work on it to be more perfect, having a balance between being and doing! With father in her mind and heart, Vishakha has to strike a realm of happiness and make her struggle for existence a worthy one.

67